Lester's
Lemon Tree

by Liza Charlesworth

ISBN: 978-1-338-89039-6

Designer: Cynthia Ng; Illustrated by John Lund

Copyright © 2023 by Liza Charlesworth. All rights reserved. Published by Scholastic Inc.

1 2 3 4 5 6 7 8 9 10   68   31 30 29 28 27 26 25 24 23 22

Printed in Jiaxing, China. First printing, January 2023.

Lester was a very nice badger.
One day, he planted a little lemon tree.
He picked the perfect spot in his backyard.
"Yay! I can watch it grow and change," he said.
And it did....

First, the little tree had lots of green leaves.

Then, it grew pretty white flowers.

Next, it grew tiny green lemons.

Last, the lemons became big
and bright and yellow.

"Yay, my lemons are ripe!" said Lester.
Lester picked the lemons and
put them in a basket.
Pluck, pluck, pluck!
Plunk, plunk, plunk!

Now, Lester had lots
of big, bright lemons.
They were lovely!
But what could he do with them?
Lester thought and thought.

Then, Lester had a great idea.
"I will invite some friends over
to see my lovely lemons!" he said.
So he sat down and made invitations.
Write, write. Draw, draw.

The next day, Lester's friends came
over to see his lemons.
"Your lemons are big and bright!" said Jill.
"Your lemons are lovely!" said Tim.
"But what can we do with them?" asked Bess.
"Hmmm, let me think about that," said Lester.

Suddenly, Lester thought of a great idea.
"We can play catch with the lemons!" he said.
Lester and Jill gave it a try.
Throw, catch. Throw, catch.
But playing catch was pretty boring.

So Lester thought of a new idea.
"We can build with the lemons," he said.
Lester and Tim gave it a try.
Build, build, build.
But the tower kept falling down.

So Lester thought of a new idea.
"We can eat the lemons!" said Lester.
Lester and Bess gave it a try.
Munch, munch…Oh, my!
The lemons were VERY sour.

Lester sat down and tried
to think of a new idea.
Think, think, think.
What could they do with
all of his lovely lemons?

Then a little butterfly flew down
and whispered in Lester's ear.
"Pssssssssssssst," she said.
"Use the lemons to make lemonade."
"What a lovely idea!" replied Lester.

First, Lester squeezed the lemons into a big pitcher.

Then, Lester added a few spoonfuls of sugar to make it sweet.

Next, Lester added ice cubes
to make it cold.

Finally, Lester poured lemonade
into five tall glasses.

"MMMMM!" said Jill, Tim, Bess, and Butterfly.
The drink was a BIG hit with his friends!
"I learned a lesson," said Lester with a grin.
"When a tree gives you lemons,
you should make lemonade!"